Selected Poems

Also by D. M. Thomas

POETRY

Modern Poets 11
Two Voices
Logan Stone
The Shaft
Love and Other Deaths
The Honeymoon Voyage
Dreaming in Bronze

TRANSLATIONS

Akhmatova:
Requiem & Poem Without a Hero
Akhmatova:
Way of All the Earth
Pushkin:
The Bronze Horseman (Selected Poems)

NOVELS

The Flute-Player
Birthstone
The White Hotel

Selected Poems

D. M. Thomas

THE VIKING PRESS   NEW YORK
PENGUIN BOOKS

Penguin Books Ltd, Harmondsworth,
Middlesex, England
Penguin Books, 625 Madison Avenue,
New York, New York 10022, U.S.A.
Penguin Books Australia Ltd, Ringwood,
Victoria, Australia
Penguin Books Canada Limited, 2801 John Street,
Markham, Ontario, Canada L3R 1B4
Penguin Books (N.Z.) Ltd, 182–190 Wairau Road,
Auckland 10, New Zealand

First published in 1983 in simultaneous hardcover and
paperback editions by The Viking Press and Penguin Books,
625 Madison Avenue, New York, New York 10022

Published simultaneously in Canada
Copyright © 1983 by D. M. Thomas
All rights reserved

LIBRARY OF CONGRESS CATALOGING IN PUBLICATION DATA
Thomas, D. M.
Selected poems.
I. Title.
PR6070.H58A6   1983   821'.914   82-10925
ISBN 0-670-70396-6 (hardbound)
ISBN 0 14 042.306 0 (paperbound)

Page 130 constitutes an extension of the copyright page.

Printed in the United States of America
Set in Garamond
Designed by Kathryn Parise

Preface

Though the two powers assume many shapes and guises, all my poems take issue with love and death. 'Sex and the dead', said Yeats, were the only two subjects worthy of a serious man's conversation, and I'd go along with that. Sex, of course, includes all creativity, and death includes its own vanquishing.

Looking back over the poetry of twenty years, I can also see, very clearly, a primary and secondary emotional landscape: Cornwall, the most westerly, Celtic outcrop of England, where I was born and grew up; and Russia, which I have encountered only through its language and literature. The atmospheric contrasts of the first—wild sea-cliffs and moors, lush river-valleys—perhaps have a counterpart in the second: Stalin and Pushkin . . .

When I was invited to make a selection of my poems, I asked for, and was generously given, the advice of friends and fellow-poets whose judgement I respect. I wish to thank Wendy Cope, Jean Driver, Ketaki K. Dyson, Diana Der Hovanessian, John Johnson, Sylvia Kantaris, and Peter Redgrove. I am grateful for this opportunity to acknowledge my debt to John Johnson: my literary agent for almost the whole of my writing life, he encouraged me before I gave him any reason to do so, and now, though formally retired, gladly consented to read and consider all of my published poetry.

However, in the end I couldn't evade the responsibility of choosing. The final test had to be whether a poem still lived, for me, however falteringly. I have also had to be conscious of the need to represent the different phases and stages of my work, and to provide as varied a selection as possible. Again, certain poems were still important to me—even though they might not work too well as poems—simply because they were crucial steps along the way.

I have grouped the poems in three sections. The first contains love poems or erotic poems; the second, poems relating to my Cornish background. The third section treats of broader themes, from history, culture, and myth. In the first two sections, the poems are printed roughly in chronological order; I have mixed them up rather more in the third.

The preference for some kind of narrative basis is already apparent in my earliest poems (e.g., 'A Lesson in the Parts of Speech' and 'Cygnus A'); and I suppose I might have foreseen (though in fact I did not) that one day I would want to write prose fiction as well as poems; or rather, poetry in the form of prose fiction. Some of the most recent poems reflect themes in my novels. I dislike rigid classification. I would like to turn back to the ancient simplicity in which any maker with words was a poet.

D. M. Thomas
November, 1981

Contents

III. Anastasia Questioned

I
The Book of Changes

Cygnus A

Removing hairgrips, nail-varnish, pensively brushing
Black hair down to the black
Bra, scattering a thick perfume on the night,
You've time to read me pointed texts
From the Gideons' Bible propped by the red-stained
       Kleenex
Till I must shut my eyes tight
While you slip
Off (still that ludicrous reserve)
Your diaphanous half-slip.

But I prefer to gaze over the dark rooftops
And talk to you over my shoulder.
Somewhere out there, love, near-neighbour Rigel
Winks its white Chaucerian light
From Orion's heel; taking its petty flight
From the peaks of the Eagle
Burning through
Hitler, by Deneb and Altair,
Falls Vega's vulturous blue;

Cambering Perseus covers half the sky,
His spring from the weeping, huddled sisters,
To see if he can reach Andromeda
Before the formless monster lands—
Cassiopeia stretches out her hands;
And out there too's the glare
Of yellow Capella
And red, bull-eyed Aldebaran.
Yet since, sweet, all my stellar

Friends are in fact outshone and liquidated
By the sun streaming from the green shade

Suspended on this window over flickers of you,
I let myself go on and on
Past Deneb, into the dark breast of the Swan
Where only the radio-
Telescope,
Picking up its grating noises,
Has any real hope

Of finding out that such a thing exists—
To a celestial catastrophe
Greater than most at various times enacted
In this Trust House—a cataclysm
Unforeseeable by their worst pessimism
—To two galaxies attracted
Into each other
At a slow thousand miles a second
Transformed to a smother

Which astronomers cannot untangle: Cygnus A.
. . . *So girlish, now that your hollow mouth*
Has shed its lipstick flavour, you hold my hand
Preventively, I kiss black hair,
Your eyes shut tight in pseudo-tragic prayer,
Your weekend penates and
My cupidon
Clutter the bedside-table beside
The white text of St John.

What must it be to have been born inside
Such a fantastic complication—
To pull aside a Cygnian tryst-house curtain
And watch the overwhelming merge

4

As whistling suns and planets all converge!
For a moment to feel uncertain
If one's discrete
Galaxy will ever emerge
With all its stars complete,

But *only* for a moment—the chances are
That not two single stars will get
Too entangled, as the run-through takes its course
In the next millennium; no glacial
Fate is ready to quench an outer-spatial
Swan-light, though scores
Of spheres sail by
Each second—blues, golds, and reds
In a greased, fabulous sky.

We're sure to see two 'silver plates' unpair
Round the Year of our Lord 90,000—
Though really, five hundred million years ago
These 'lovers' fled away, despite
Curiosity at Jodrell Bank tonight;
No doubt by this time snow
Has covered over
Many a planet, and Judgement-Day
Has heard the excuse of lovers:

'But that was in another galaxy,
And besides, the star is dead!'
While on live red-dwarfs, others will see St John
Shine in your eyes, an aeon hence,

Recording, with their brilliant instruments,
That the red-shift heaven's undergone
So shyly, doesn't veil
Completely the Magellanic Cloud,
Though all space-trips fail.

A Lesson in the Parts of Speech

Loraine (my Proper but improper darling),
with all these chalked and innocent-eyed Abstractions,
with fear, desire, with jealousy, with pain,
I love
the things about you (Common but uncommon),
eyes, lips, hair, fingers, breasts and smiles and bottom,
blouse, skirt, suspenders, sweater, stockings, shoes

—for they are You, my one and only pronoun,
my slyly Personal, my unpossessed Possessive!
How queerly You, Demonstrative last night,
can sit, now, lost among your friends, Indefinite,

silent, anonymous, maddening, discreet,
concentrated, withdrawn from me, allowing
just the subtlest smile to play as I write up 'red',
our private joke; your genial body purrs
as you stretch your heavy limbs, back in the desk,
tight as a nun, arms folding warm to chest,
reserved, self-owned, and taking notes though bored.

Deep in the past, last night, we clung, we kissed,
tangled, confused the first and second person,
petted, then did your homework, frenchkissed again,
though when it came to the final, explosive verb,
you shut your self, in passive mood, and tense;
and seeing you in the class,
inviolate in fresh school-blouse, so serenely
escaping always into the future, the finite
so impossible to make infinitive,
in impotent, baffled fury I would plunge

wantonly, completely, here, now,

in through up under unto and beyond
above relationship of place or time or . . .

But
(and this our accepted, clean and cold conjunction,
the word that separates us and attracts us)

all is determined in our complex sentence.
The bars of our open prisons call us back
from our brief, touching forays to the woods,
where planned ejaculations missed their mark.
You look up, meet my eyes. Heart thumps like a gong.
Your gaze is tender, teasing, swift. Mine says:
and oh! and oh! and oh!
till that time come again . . .
and yours: *hey nonny nonny!*

Wolfbane

It was not
by any of the usual
signs by

merged brows
haired palms
pointed ears
reddening of eyes
             in the moon

or her undressed
body's
disappearance
in the silver
mirror

but by the way her mind
under him
turned away
loping
into snowy
darkness

From *Computer 70:*
Dreams & love poems

12

Be great to fuck you on the dunes
where nothing grows but dry sandgrass,
your face a wayside stone of runes.

Lit by the headlights and the moon's
our instants throng on us and pass.
Be great to fuck you on the dunes.

Hand groping thigh, the future swoons
like a nude patient under gas;
your face a wayside stone of runes.

Midnight and engine-warmth maroons
us on Steel Island ringed by glass.
Be great to fuck you on the dunes.

Viola-husked the engine croons
monotones enigmatic as
your face. A wayside stone of runes

flicks by; the sharp rear-mirror prunes
from glare of might-be drifts of was.
Be great to fuck you on the dunes,
your face a wayside stone of runes.

13
I

This final privacy:
in love or war
to be shot
surrounded by cameramen.

Wait! Freeze.
A camera-plate is broken.
A fly settles on sweat.

II

Colour-supplement
for a grey sunday;
concentratedly,
staring down, this vietnamese
girl, man-handled, does up her
shirt-button;
her bewildered, lively, almost-
dead child on her arm.
It is
obscene of her.
No one should be shot
fastening a shirt-button
ten seconds before being shot,
(triangle of firm brown flesh).

14

I watch you, glacial in mink,
enter on the arm of your husband,
imperious through the sighs
of your fans, the autographs.
Haughty, you take your seat;
your arm shrinks from his hand;
I whisper into your ear,

I am still crazy for you.
    Mink is as tender as steel
    in alphaville.

He is still crazy for you.
He watches you, late, uncombed,
with lateness on your mind
straight from your doctor's room,
enter the cinema's dark
afternoon, sit straight by him.
Neither yet flickers a sign.
You brush your hair from your eyes.
    Hair is as molten as steel
    in alphaville.

He watches you watching the screen
with never a glance at him.
He watches him loving you,
je t'aime je t'aime je t'aime
he whispers, now as then.
He is still crazy for you.
Your hands touch on the sheet,
like pack-ice, split again.
    Days are as cool as steel
    in alphaville.

Love is a cutting-room, all
images equally true,
I mix them all up in you,
au revoir becomes *je t'aime*
in the crystal at your ear,
as I direct your hand

to stretch for husband, lover;
the camera is crazy for you.
 A film can be cut like steel
 in alphaville.

Your hands in the pit of your back,
steel grapples to eyes of steel;
your breasts on hoardings star;
swiftly you brush your hair;
your husband is crazy for you.
Our son must be fetched from school.
Blinds of the late afternoon
are falling one by one.
 Light opens on the steel
 evening of alphaville.

From *Haiku Sequence*

With time to spare. Your
pleased turned-away languor
pleases me. Slow thaw.

Prevented, re-tracing spine,
lips find that blizzards
have buried tracks.

Delighted tongue ravishing
your ear wears like all
males a crude sheath.

House of Bernarda Alba.
Absorbing, cloistral.
Vulva without doors.

Ear deep-tongued: if
my brain had a Bartholin's gland
it would be flooded.

You extract a wet
clinging hair from your mouth:
snake biting its own tail.

His engorgement,
this climbing stretchmark,
unbroken vertical.

I'd live gladly off
your five exudations,
those loaves and fishes.

Ten fingers join hands, dance
in the stifling-hot,
resting arena.

Teeth clamped to my nipple,
you stir
lust out of anger.

Lacquered nail, cold, indulgent,
pierces the anus:
a queen in Soho.

Thighs grip as they lose
the river they will
not wade in twice.

Light from receding
galaxies can't keep
pace with itself.

Tell her the stain
on your dress came
from gathering whitecurrants.

Flecked with red, a white-
packed ashtray invokes
your late guest.

Unreal. In the train
I lift my finger to smell
your faint fingerprint.

Our cigarette afterglows
in car window.
Star-shower from Capricorn.

Seventeen wild strokes.
So much passion needs
your quiet scabbard.

Trawl

O fisher-girl,
when the shoal is brought in,
the rich white harvest
leaping and dying on the shore,
and beginning to give off
the smell of decay,
your shoulderblades
pale hungry fins
turn away,
your long, wading thighs
silently weep.

Lakeside

'*Prove that you love me!*' she said, as a girl will.
'*Anything!*' the boy stammered. '*Anything? Then let me see
you walk the waves.*' He fished for inspiration in her eyes.
And walked. She gave him the spice of her lips, half-mockingly.

'*Prove that you love me! Change this water into wine.*'
She pointed to her pitcher, cracked in the heat of noon.
He lifted an arm. She drank, and hugged her ankles.
Game him the wine of her tongue, and bit his own.

'*Prove that you love me!*' '*Anything.*' '*I'm hungry now.
Change this dry crust to a feast, and don't be long.*'
There were baskets to spare. She bared her small teeth in pleasure.
Spared him the roes her breasts—then away she sprang.

Hid herself in a rock. Tortured, he seized her.
But she wriggled like a lizard away. '*Prove
that you love me!*' A cripple was passing. '*Heal me him.*'
The cripple walked. For an instant his finger clove

the hill of frankincense, but again she twisted
out of his grasp, her laugh invaded by a gasp of pain.
She stood on the rock, goading, belly thrust forward.
'*Prove that you love me! Die for me,*' she said.

'*Die, and you can have this. Not unless.*' She kilted
her robe, pulled open the sepulchre to show the red
sand-flesh waiting. Speech and colour left his lips.
'*So you* don't *love me!*' She laughed, spat grossly, and fled.

Wandering to the shore, he helped the fishermen
with their nets; but his mind and his blood ran

on the frightening fount of energy that had leapt in him.
She bitched about homelong, blood splashing like menstrual wine

that flowered lemon-trees in her aimless wake;
forgot by dusk the strange shy clumsy boy,
knowing too well the power in her little finger
to stir such deeds, and more, when the devil was in her.

Logan Stone

if it were one
stone it would not be magical
if it were two stones   the attrition of
rain cutting into its natural weakness too well
it would not be magical   if its massif could be set
trembling   neither two nor one   for a moment only   say
the logging-point of night-fall it would be magical yet
not miraculous   small worlds may be born of such magic
but that it can go on and on   without ceasing   dazzling
the spectator with motionless motion neither two nor one
neither one nor two doomed and unshakable on its point
of infinity that is the miracle   to be so weak
a finger logs it   what constant strength
what force it takes to be a
logan
stone you and I what cold applied
granite-fire logging on weakness no storm can move us

Friday Evening

You are on the train crawling across country towards me.
I am in the car driving to a half-way station.
You are switching on the overhead reading-light.
I am switching on the car sidelights.
You are losing yourself in a book.
I am losing myself in a poem.
I know this road like the palm of your hand.
To give up is as desperate as to go on.
You lean your head on the glass, speckling with rain like sperm.
I switch on the wipers.
Dusk deepens.
The station will always be there to meet us,
Unable to go even when the last train is in,
Even when the sun flickers low, a waiting-room fire.

You Are on Some Road

The evening star
trembling in blue light

The red star
breaking through the dusk
like acetylene

The Orion stars
blossoming
like desert flowers

Even the Pleiads
sharply visible
like children in white
on a dark street

Tribes of stars
never seen before
drumming beyond the drift
of the Coal Sack

You are on some road

From *Sonoran Poems*

I descend I enter you
a diplomat sick of negotiations
choosing to be hijacked
by a blue stewardess
with a gun instead of champagne

in the midst of a ghost-town
in the midst of a desert
to rest
to forget time and the six
directions to be forgotten

Like a kachina-mask
you wear your beauty like a kachina-mask
      your beauty

the minute you are gone
    desert rain
        red
        mariposa lilies
        astonished
        mariposa lilies

From desert scrub the lord's candles glimmer
a wind shivers and I am changed

without knowing it yet
without holding it yet
mistaking it for joy

I become good
I become loyal to myself

moment by moment
new stars made

O Mother of Tonantsin
O Our Lady of Guadalupe

The bulb-light flickers
figures are there searching
combing the ghost-town

You stand with blue lips
back to the door
alien and fanatic
covering me

But how can love recede
but how can love recede
those slit domes
through which the night keeps pouring

It is my kachina-mask
it is my kachina-mask
instead of patched jeans
you come to me dressed
as the traditional spy
and seducer quelling your nature
it is my birthday you say

long black gloves
garterbelt and stockings
tense as a strung bow

I fuck it as I pretend
it is you I fuck
it is the fetish I fuck
it is the god
the mountain around which
everything moves it is here
and here and here
in these fulcra of greatest anguish

I adore the oppugnant stresses
agent and double agent and triple agent

wearing my kachina-mask
I will betray anything
wearing my kachina-mask

You
the song
bring a smile to my lips
I cannot silence

Muse you are dead
why do you walk along my dreams
my dry veins
hunting your murdered children
and wailing and scratching huge rents
in the backs of lost travellers
like the ghost-woman of the sandflats of the Santa Cruz

I am tired of faces
that shine next to me as close

as a filling station the other side a motorway
softly shining
at night

Let the downpour be stored

My soul is very lonely
blind he has touched your face
he sends me to be a go-between
to beg you to come

bring a flower of the saguaro cactus
to cure my friend

The Indian cemetery at Xan Xavier
square and facing east
their white and nameless crosses

your hand gently enchaining me
and your eyes with love releasing me
it is not of death I think
on this happy day
but as if the whole universe moves towards the east

From *The Book of Changes*

Parched, they drink
each other,
from a
single glass
clouded with the
fallout of mountains.

Not snow,
but wind
through the
branches. She holds
her white
skirt down.

Her so
pliable limbs
are singing like
cherry branches
overwhelmed by
the wind.

She gashes open,
tangy, moist,
a great
fruit that
has not
been eaten.

He is mounted.
The whole earth
beyond horizons is
his. Blue haze
of distance charms
his tenant's house.

She wears
a yellow
shift like
an orchard.
She treads
on hoarfrost.

Thunder is
felt through
floor and soles.
The white fence
is entangled in
a ram's horns.

Her thighs,
his thighs, her
hands again
in the
centre. It is
all flowing.

Or his thighs,
her thighs,
his hands again
in the centre.
It is
all clinging brightness.

She becomes
the muscle of
the calf. He
becomes the springing
movement of
the foot.

She trails
her empty
basket home. She
has eaten
the berries meant
for the boilingpan.

His mouth cannot
impose his
will. He is
a talking
traveller in a
carriage of ghosts.

Life is
being drawn even
from the
wells to which
the birds no
longer come.

Caresses by
the mild tiger
at his shoulder
are changing all
the skin
of his body.

Her breath
growing faster,
she is
a village girl

ascending into a
great city.

She recalls
their son,
benighted somewhere far
off, very
near. Thunder-
stroke after stroke.

His head
tilts back. It
is getting dark.
He must
enter his
house and rest.

Their bodies have
drowned together. Across
a wind-
shaken lake
he is rowing
an empty boat.

Wet from head
to tail
a young fox,
a red
salmon, is crossing
the river.

Flesh

Let me ache, indicate, simper who touched
your warm cunt, whisper, let on now,
disperse them into our love.
Who did you? it's all the same:
deep pricks or, islands of assiduous fictions,
disperse them into our love.

Am I in her, pummel her, he fucked you, ah
total and thousands of indecent, poked it in
did he, turgid and slewed, my girl, you right
there immixed with another, convoke it actually
wrapt round him, feel his engorgement
displacing your space, cleaving your achable
cleft better than this, novel then sweetly
a habit, why that's my spirit,
my fluttering clairvoyant, my fat ghost.

Weddings

GIRLS

Churning it in up tight you wean us: come serve it us can't
sing in rhythm, O take us, extend it, we're fir-cones ignited,
stick hurt us, wide in, out, permit it here, exhilarate,
noon tomorrow exile you weary, we can't look at our parents.

I means us, henceforward, I means us!

YOUTHS

Penetrate quite all, we're men now and in labour,
nose and eye O mingled, alive who can divide us or release?
Those with worried minds, salt them, commit them to boxes.
Stickier, jam, you sip, a hint, respond it, hairy, lick a bit.

I means us, henceforward, I means us!

GIRLS

Yes but quick we'll offer to, it's crude but, our rings on,
so why not, our mothers' complexions must have caught fire
too, our reticent mothers, the birth-cleft levels us,
eat, you wean us, go further, we're casting up ashore.

I means us, henceforward, I means us!

YOUTHS

Yes but look hello your cunts are a bush-fire,
we're not yet old enough to beat down the flames,
where's the white pepper stars you blew in your parents' eyes?

We're not sure pray us where we should tool it, harder,
wide ought we or dive us feel we sick or rotate us, whores?

GIRLS

Yes spear us no peace can equal it tool it you name

.   .   .   .

YOUTHS

Our one idea now's a sleepy reversion.
What love is we know not but that its question
you've quickened us to ask,
now quiet our minds require no answer.

.   .   .   .

GIRLS

What flowers inside us in secret
                              is plighted to hurt us,
convulse us all through, notice already our breast-bites.
Ride then, come tenderly, deflower us again we're hungry,
seek the virgins that stay in us intact, carry them away,
cover us as you promised with flowers of pollution,
graze in us, you can't have meant it, but careful, pool all this.

I means us, henceforward, I means us!

YOUTHS

Gentle though, prone on us, summon us, yes but slowly,
ankles now up to our hips, no lie we're trees, see you win.

32

Drink too the pungent jugs, tails, on our lips, virgins,
nothing's repugnant to equal it, why your fathers did tipsy
their lips with your mothers, those quibblers paired closest,
all their virginity's toasted, your parents are adepts,
third part of their lives was threshing, the pattering seeds,

GIRLS

and we're now the sun's toast: lip your hairy dew on us
quick penetrate our ass milk drummed out and simultaneous.

I means us, henceforward, I means us!

Two Women,
Made by the Selfsame Hand

Each day I'd come back to the statuette,
the boy-girl, sturdy, nude, her elfin head
turned to the right, rejecting, yet
teasingly tilted; sensual and sad;
I'd touch my wallet, let it go; her hand
offered with upturned palm what it concealed.
She'd laugh at my uncertainty, and stand
admiringly before a Mother and Child:

—my friend, I mean; my more than friend. Our days
of rainy holiday were haunted by
a girl with briny locks and changeling gaze,
the left hand open on her thigh,
late-adolescent undine perching on
a rock—and her soulful primitive
madonna, tall and standing, gazing down
with all the fear that perfect love can give.

One hand sustained, the other curved around
the shell that held the whole of life, too brittle.
Oh but she wanted it! and would have found
the money for it, if *he* were not so little,
if his curious little hands weren't everywhere . . .
I watched her fade back through her gaze to hug
the absent child who is always there.
He'd break it, wouldn't he? . . . I shrugged

away her unbearable, unexpressed
question, and saw how disappointingly
the nude had changed again; the small pert breasts
and rounded thighs still pulled, but yesterday
her face was not so coarse nor so

34

malign, the fingers playing with a strand
more natural. I left the studio
for the last time, downcast; but looked back and

the girl was following; she wanted me
to have her, she said; her upturned palm
gestured with such a brazen subtlety,
her delicate grieving features held such charm,
I paused by the harbour, strode back, and got her.
She laughed at my confusion, glanced farewell
obliquely at the other terra-cotta,
followed me, and we drove to our hotel,

where doubts are cast aside: she draws my soul
into her numinous clay; our mingled smoke
broods on the irresponsible
tilted head under lamplight as we joke
about that open, all-accepting hand
hiding her sex. I say it means, *how much?* . . .
It means, she says, *get stuffed* . . . We undress and
lie down as straight as effigies. I touch

at length her hand, her closed thighs, the uncouth
wires I prise apart, as mad for her
as in her playful and affectionate youth.
She tilts away her head, and does not stir.
I turn her mouth to mine, but it stays lax.
I hear the sisters talking in her blood,
the nurturing madonna without sex,
the lonely mistress without motherhood.

They greet across my flesh, across the bay
between the studio and our hotel bed.

Almost before I've pulled away
she's lit a cigarette, her sculpted head
talks to itself in a calm monotone;
the hands, she says, of neither piece are right;
the hands . . . the hands are wrong . . . I lie like stone,
hearing her cut deep fractures from the night.

Poetry and Striptease

Poetry and Striptease, said the London Entertainments Guide;
but when I flipped to that heart-stunning page,
the Soho strip-clubs weren't offering poetry,
and the Poetry Society wasn't offering striptease.

I didn't want the sepulchre of Eros,
huddled with mourners before waxen corpses;
I didn't want to clap with poetasters
the severed head of Orpheus in Earls Court;

in a packed East End pub I drowned my sorrow,
loathing the spill of beer, the reek of breaths,
the vapid babble, brawny men, pale wives—
till from a side-room I heard raucous music.

The young strip-artist was already naked, splayed;
borrowing a bitter and rubbing the froth in,
she caught the drips in the glass, and offered it
with a smile back to the man, to taste, to taste.

He recoiled in disgust; it was too hot a cargo
for these dockers to handle, and they gasped and guffawed
their nausea, yet craned, and stared in awe, as if
at a banana-spider in a crate; as if

this rosy girl with the dark pubic tuft
dripping like woodland foliage after rain
was Salome dancing with the Baptist's head;
even the blacks in our dense standing circle

paled at the gash the strangely innocent girl
was smearing with white. Like great black trees

they swayed away; at the same time their stare
grew rooted in her, as did mine; and when

she put the glass down and resumed her dance,
the writhing girl, straining far back, became
only a medium for what her nakedness
still veiled; and there was nothing in the room

except that hypnotising gash, a part of her
and yet apart; we saw our lives, our deaths;
supported on her hands, her thighs spread wide,
running with sweat, she turned an arc, and gazed

down, with a smile, yet curiously, wistfully,
at the black jolting mound, as if to say—
'I don't know what it is, or where it goes;
it's a rose in a glass, my semi-transparent soul;

it's the place where I have to dance . . .'
She swayed it like a flute, like the foaming wave
ahead of Venus, wading from the sea—
poetry and striptease, striptease and poetry.

From *Don Giovanni*

One evening when the lake was a red sheet,
we dressed, and climbed up to the mountain peak
behind the white hotel, up the rough path
zig-zagging between larches, pines, his hand
helped me in the climb, but also swayed
inside me, seeking me. When we had gained
the yew trees by the church we rested there;
grazing short grass, a tethered donkey stared,
an old nun with a basket of soiled clothes
came, as he glided in, and said, The cold
spring here will take away all sin,
don't stop. It was the spring that fed the lake
the sun drew up to fall again as rain.
She washed the clothes. We scrambled up the slope
into the region of eternal cold
above the trees. The sun dropped, just in time,
we entered the observatory, blind.
I don't know if you know how much your son
admires the stars, the stars are in his blood,
but when we gazed up through the glass there were
no stars at all, the stars had gone to earth;
I didn't know till then the stars, in flakes
of snow, come down to fuck the earth, the lake.
It was too dark to reach the white hotel
that night, and so we fucked again, and slept.
I felt the ghostly images of him
cascading, and I heard the mountains sing,
for mountains when they meet sing songs like whales.

The whole night sky came down that night, in flakes,
we lay in such high silence that we heard
the joyful sighs of when the universe

began to come, so many years ago,
at dawn when we crunched stars to drink the snow
everything was white, the lake as well,
the white hotel was lost, until he turned
the glass down towards the lake and saw the words
I'd written on our window with my breath.
He moved the glass and we saw edelweiss
rippling in a distant mountain's ice,
he pointed where some parachutists fell
between two peaks, we saw the sunlight flash
in the now heavenly blue, a corset clasp,
it was our friend, there was the lilac bruise
his thumb had printed in her thigh, the sight
excited him I think, my light
head felt him burst up through, the cable car
hung on a strand, swung in the wind, my heart
was fluttering madly and I screamed, the guests
fell through the sky, his tongue drummed at my breast,
I've never known my nipples grow so quickly,
the women fell more slowly, almost drifting,
because their petticoats and skirts were galing,
the men fell through them, my heart was breaking,
the women seemed to rise not fall, a dance
in which the men were lifting in light hands
light ballerinas high above their heads,
the men were first to come to ground, and then
the women fell into the lake or trees,
silently followed by a few bright skis.

On our way down we rested by the spring.
Strangely from so high we saw the fish
clearly in the lucid lake, a million

gliding darting fins of gold or silver
reminding me of the sperm seeking my womb.
Some of the fish were nuzzling guests for food.
Am I too sexual? I sometimes think
I am obsessed by it, it's not as if
God fills the waters with mad spawning shapes
or loads the vine with grapes, the palm with dates,
or makes the bull dilate to take the peach
or the plum tremble at the ox's reek
or the sun cover the pale moon. Your son
crashed through my modesty, a stag in rut.
The staff were wonderful. I've never known
such service as they gave, the telephones
were never still, nor the reception bell,
honeymoon couples, begging for a bed,
had to be turned away, as guests moved out
a dozen more moved in, they found
a corner for a couple we heard weeping
at being turned away, we heard her screaming
somewhere the next night, the birth beginning,
waiters and maids were running with warm linen.
The burnt-out wing was built again in days,
the staff all helped, one morning when my face
lay buried in the pillow, and my rump
taking his thrusts was coming in a flood
we heard a scraping, at the window was
the jolly chef, his face was beaming, hot,
he gave the wood a fresh white coat, and winked,
I didn't mind which one of them was in,
the steaks he cooked were rare and beautiful,
the juice was natural, and it was good
to feel a part of me was someone else,

no one was selfish in the white hotel
where waters of the lake could lap the screes
of mountains that the wild swans soared between,
their down so snowy-white the peaks seemed grey,
or glided down between them to the lake.

Blizzard Song

On black ice,
lady of secrets,
girl of grey eyes,
we passed each other.

Lady of secrets,
your eyes flicked aside;
we passed each other
but I meant nothing to you.

Your eyes flicked aside
between your upturned collar,
but I meant nothing to you,
you were rushing.

Between your upturned collar
your cheeks were two flames;
you were rushing
to your lover;

your cheeks were two flames,
you were bringing heat
to your lover;
passers-by warmed themselves;

you were bringing heat,
scattering snow;
passers-by warmed themselves,
smiling through white stars.

Scattering snow,
you stand in his porch,
smiling through white stars
as you slide your coat off;

you stand in his porch,
with the blizzard's song;
as you slide your coat off
we move into one, spinning

with the blizzard's song,
girl of grey eyes,
we move into one, spinning
on black ice.

II
The Handkerchief or Ghost Tree

Penwith

Did flint tools or alone the driving rain
complete its holy paradox: granitic
yet sensitive as the joint of a bone?

Nine maidens petrified for sabbath dancing
or sun-discs crouched in an altar-less ring,
in a misty field the sea's whetstone hones
to a sharp blade; the sun tests it, aslant.

On the humped moor's spine, consumptive miners
turned aside from their plod home to crouch and pass
through the men-an-tol, the ring of granite.

I am the logan stone a cloud can alter,
inert mass trembling on a compass-point;
I am the men-an-tol, the wind's vagina;
I am the circle of stones grouped around grass.

Botallack

Needles flake off into the blue air. Listen.
In the August silence, on the bare cliff-path, you can fling
a stone and it will not break the silence, but you can hear
the wedges and drills of erosion hammering
in a silence that is uproar, beneath the wrecking Brissons.

The sea might ring to a finger today. Bone-china.
Without the drama of weathers, no flowers or trees
to mask time with recurrence, time's raw nerve
shows through here like an outcrop of tin. A peace
that is the acceptance of defeat reigns. Miners

trekked this vertical, nerves tempered granite;
at their head, candles — defeat — disaster — dowsed,
to stride out under the sea as courageous,
poor in all but tall tales the ocean housed,
as their methodist Christ walked out upon it.

Botallack locks against too strong a force;
blue-framed, nettled engine-house, cliff-set. The logan stone
of me is here. Bal-maidens spalling ore
for bread feared not the plunge. Why should I alone
stride ahead of the flood, on a white sea-horse?

Down in those spirit-heights, if the guttering
candles failed, kind-
ly light amidst the encircling gloom, one man
guided them unfailingly through blackwaters. He was blind.
In the country of the blind, that man was king.

From *Meditation on Lines from the Methodist Hymnal*

the seed-time and the harvest

'But naturally!' laughs the out-of-work analyst.
'You are seeking the boy you never were.' Sails rest,
temporary as butterflies, on the estuary. I have confessed
I usually fall for women with small breasts.
Shouting it out; for he is deaf as a post.

and pour contempt on all my pride

Out of the blue of the scudding land's end sky,
in my second, dodging, darkglassed holiday,
five miners slouch down the seaward way,
croust-bags swinging, towards old Geevor mine. 'They
must be pot-holers.' Reddled with their trade, eyes and
teeth cheerily
gleam. We pull in to see.
They stare at the tourists staring at them. I look away.
The guidebook says: 'they heard the seabed stones rattle
above their gallery.'
Converted to a meadery,
a gaunt Wesleyan chapel. We sit
by scented fingerbowls and candlelight
in bottles, crouched over barreltops, and eat
scampi and chips, drink the honeymoon drink. A glint
of family madness in her eyes, my love talks about
dying. 'Fuck death!' I spit,
and slide my hand along the pew, under her skirt.
Invasive as a celtic saint,
my finger opens her like the spine of a new testament.

and glory shone around

The granite shoulder of the penwith moor wears heather
purple as the cloak of Joseph of Arimathea
when he rode on muleback up from the island harbour,
the 'hoar rock in the woods'; the young ship's carpenter
riding beside him. They came to stare

at the blackrobed barbarians streaming the precious ore.
A grey fist with a raised index finger,
the ruined engine-house of Ding-Dong mine still stands there
today high on the jagged height of the pagan moor.
We have bruised the heather to stare
at men-an-tol, holed stone in the ground: curer
of scrofula, barrenness, broken heart, or wart.
Though it says naked, in the guidebook, stuff that.
Clothed as I am, I'll squat
and squirm through it.

where shall Seined by a million bones,
my wandering my soul begins
soul begin here in the stamping-house of bronze.

rock of ages At Botallack. The engine-house of the knackt bal
cleft for me overleans the cliff-edge. More beautiful,
even, than before man's depredation brought toil
and scars to this loneliest wild heel
of Cornwall. Blue day, winds from the murderous Brissons flail
her light dress, my shirt. The sea folds and unfurls
endlessly its spray. Ancestral
miners trail
before and behind us down the gullhewn perilous
path, vanish underground undersea. Bal-
maidens surround us, spall
the ore with long hammers. They loved their hammered hailed
rock. Their love was need. It failed.
Lies like kerensa beyond recall,
like the makers of the cromlechs on the hill.
From failure is this beauty born. My girl
blends with the chough-calls her light southern drawl.

Our passing call
has changed Botallack, brings a new love, however frail,
to overlay kerensa. The tidal pull
brings new lives in like wrecks, as hedges fall
away to sea. The celts were strangers. Our fingers spall,
in unison, ore beyond bronze. No alloy is final.

Cecie

The evening that you died was the first I could not
Overhear you bed-down with your 'dear Nellie':
No farting and whispering. The house lay cursed
Not with one death only: with its own.
Who, you asked in my head, will lace my brother's
Shoes up in the morning, empty the chamberpots
And dress my sister? There was no reply.
I heard you struggle to sit up in the coffin.
You'd have worked all night and worked off that deep hurt.

Dear aunt, if Christ had come, as well he might, to you,
You'd have scrubbed his feet with good soapy water
Left from Monday's wash, pocketed a few
Fresh loaves and fishes for your poor sister;
Burnt your hand on the boiler, muttered, 'That's nothin'',
Run out, lisle stocking flapping, to dig the garden.

You demand—clucking at the grave in such a state,
From our habit of taking you for granted—shears,
Scrubbing-brush, water, not for your sake but hers
You lie beside again. An image of you: triangle:
Lawn, mower and you (no taller than it)
Leaning a force three times your fleshless weight.
70, your death shocked us like a child's.

In all but stoicism you *were* a child.
Rampaging through the village you never left,
Blackberry-faced, hot pasties in your apron,
Scuttling, chuckling. No breasts to hold or suck at.

You had no life. No lovers that I know of.
Yet we all loved you. You were filled with love

No one repaid. Death can't be a still
Nor a cobwebbed house any longer, full of your labour,
Farting, scurrying. You have no death.
So much living is living still.

Reticent

How they loved understatement!
'Goin' a' drop rain, are us?'—the sky
an enraged bladder. 'He've had a drop to drink.'
'I dear like bit ride'—those grotesque tea-treat safaris
to Weston-super-Mare or Timbuctoo,
with a break for drop tea and a brisk turn
round the amazement-arcades before starting back.
'Nice few taties this year, 'n?' 'Nice bit o' meat, plenty
for all of us.' 'He've got a shillin' in his purse'
—John Jago with his Johannesburg gold-shares.
'Are you goin' to kiss me? 'Cause you're goin' away
for a few minutes'—I to my Oxford term.
It expressed their landscape;
deep labyrinths under the shafted bracken.

Now a drop of rain drums on a good few graves.
Plenty enough for me.
Some with not even a jampot to catch it.
When I've had a drop to drink
I can bear my mother's lonely, painful descent;
'You're not looking too bad.'
Cursed with the style, I felt embarrassed to
bend and kiss my father's tortured face,
he 'no better' behind the corner screen,
he going away for a few minutes.
Liking bit ride, I drive 200 miles
to glance at my watch till it's time to go again.
Without exaggeration the landscape weeps.
I've got a shilling but I can't spend it.

Dream

My woman said to me
I feel so guilty
at never knowing your father

    why don't you let him
    come and fetch me on sunday
    for the big easter tea at your house
    instead of you?

        And have him come early
        then he can sleep with me
        if you don't mind

    Mind! I was very pleased and excited
    easter day parties at our house
    are terribly grim with the dead
    still in their grave clothes & still dying
    & just a cup of potato wine

When I met him from the cemetery
it was wonderful
to see him so much better & younger
so wiry & healthy &
filthy dirty from work & his carroty
hairtufts I'd forgotten
making his whole body glow like an indian brave

    but when it came to it
    I didn't like to ask him
    if he'd fetch my woman

        because he'd forgotten the letter f
        & fourteen years of death
        makes driving strange & dangerous

it might seem I was taking advantage
I couldn't be open with him

and he

humble as always reticent
he didn't want to seem pushing

Rubble

I sit in my mother's cramped bedsit,
on edge in body and spirit.
The light too bright for her eyes.
The radio too loud for her ears.
The low fire too hot for her
seized limbs appalling me.

Yet she wants to live.
Yet to rejoin her husband.
To win, lose, tie, go on running.

Almost it is a quarter to nine
when I can jump up, heat
her milk and water, kettle
for her bottle, pull out the commode,
compel myself to kiss her, and go.

She is a fledgling
broken on the road
I want to be out of sight of.
But alive, or the world will fold.

It is as though the black hole
drawing her into itself
is conditioning my love
to require absence. She knows

it. She is content. There is
a queer radiance in the space
between us which my eyes
avoid occupying: the radium
Madame Curie found, when desolate
she returned at night to the empty table.

Ninemaidens

(Stone-circle, West Cornwall)

Our sorrow and our joy
Dance with us.
Nine maidens
We are unaccountable.

Dance with us
The sabbath-dances.
We are unaccountable
For this summer lightning.

The sabbath dances
Astonished,
For this summer lightning
Is love.

Astonished
Our hearts thunder.
Is love
Anything but yes?

Our hearts thunder
With desire for you.
Anything but yes
And we should die.

With desire for you
We are struck dumb.
And we should die
In your arms.

We are struck dumb,
Having too many words.
In your arms
Stone is beautiful.

Having too many words
We close into a circle.
Stone is beautiful.
We open to you.

We close into a circle,
Ninemaidens.
We open to you
Our sorrow and our joy.

A Cornish Graveyard at Keweenaw
(N. Michigan)

Harriet Uren, 100, eighty years from Penzance,
Died with the scent of saffron in the cloam.
Daughter and great-grandmother, felt death enter
Like the slow dark voyage down the home coast.
Plymouth was strange, Fowey less; she could not weep
Though grown men wept, as hymn on hymn unrolled
The Lizard, flashing. Then the Mount, the light,
Only a miner's daughter could have seen,
Drawing away as she drew nearer home.

Turned then, bride to groom, and went below.
Undressed in the dense dark, too shy to breathe.
Surrendered to what might come, her eyes chatoyant,
Rocked in fusions
Of gain and loss and that sustaining rise.
Praying only this night what may suffice,
She slept. Couples embrace, weep, talk,
Or sleep. On deck, the Scillies past, the seethe
Of brotherly harmony grows coarse and buoyant.

And here intuited their second life.
That granite outcrop grew them, this grew with them.
Cherished rock more than they cherished flesh, drilled,
Blasted it, as they went, sang as they went.
Stillness in this boomed peninsular
Unrest. Yet so much, and such dry, Cornish
Wit, together! Such eager harmonies
To such handsome voices keen to pitch a tune!
Praise God for the water's lap, the same horn-thrust.

And all in time who went on to unlock
Nevadan silver, Californian gold,

Great pranksters, wrestlers and evangelists,
Wondered before they died or slept
Which was their home, Cornwall or Keweenaw.
The seams of want and wanderlust
Compelled new shafts of love, but those clairvoyant
And helmet eyes still saw a celtic cross
And window-light, their roots their albatross.

Sumach sighs, and the great lake locks in ice.
You are luminescent with impurities,
Tarnished with fractures, silky with inclusions,
Your winks and laughter ride out circumstance,
You prod each other with ironic fists.
Tin into gold, my sonnies, my alchemists.
You who're quicksilver like New Almadén—
Where now? Impossible you'll stay in baulk,
With that swift talk, in pulses, like your sea.

Decks crammed like troopships, or pared, two
By two, hard-rock miners driving into talc,
Ricepaper clinging to honeymoon silk.
I praise God's ship of death, restorative,
Hiding the bone, healing the lung's scar,
And imagine what Liberty has hushed their dry
Expanding stories awhile, their souls raw,
Their eyes bright, moving west across the spectrum
Of hard rock, giving new land new energy.

From *Under Carn Brea*

MONA

Mona turned all language to a comic
Amazement at catastrophe barely averted.
'My *gar*, Harold! What did you *do*?'
Round eyes puckering to chuckles at a new
Panic and wonder, 'My *life*,
HARold!' Left every phrase on the rise
Dazzled in its natural drama.

Nothing happened at the creek
That week each summer. I was puzzled
Why parents didn't need to play, just laugh
In tune with Mona's anguished shrieks
At Harry's bloodies and buggers as he guzzled
The fish he'd caught. The lamp lit,
Harry in bed, Mona did exercises,

Groaned, bumped and thumped, showed how far
Snapped suspenders sank back in the fat.
'I'n it shameful!' Whooped her anguish.
'Mona you're obscene.' Kneaded more flesh,
Found more. 'AMy!' chuckled and thumped. 'My *gar*!
Harold, did you *ever*!' I understood,
Half-asleep in my mother's lap,
Everything aquiver, it was good.

HAROLD

When you laughed, at your own joke or another's,
To the damned and God himself it carried.
Which came back to you, amplifying your laughter.

God shook then over all the wheatfields.
Making you throw your head back and split the ceiling.
God suffered agonies in his own chapels.
Back went your head, blasting the rooftops.
If it rained it was God's helpless tears.

BEN WEARNE

'Think of his dear mother, she could 'ardly stan', crawlin'
About on 'er 'ands and knees, I expec' she was,
Beatin' 'er 'ead on the ground, 'cause 'er *dear Son*,
'Er dear *cheel*, was in *hagony*' (here his tears
Would well). 'How could hanybody *do* it to'n?

Look at'n there, upon the cross of glory,
His poor hands and feet, the dear of'm, the *dear* of'm . . .'
He made it sound not like an old story,
But like a real son—his own son.

Well, he is dead, I suppose, though I never heard,
And, I suppose, his native carn his cairn.
I hope they sent him off with his own tune, Blaenwaern.

SUNDAY EVENING

Eddie hovering, searching for one last loud
Chord, closing his eyes in bliss,
Hearing it fade in my father's soulful ending.
Leslie unveiling his score, a touch of class,
A refining fire, to his wife's ivory smile

Like a mild orgasm. Finger to lowered brow,
Retired Eddie's expressionless wink

At whoever caught his expression.
Cecie scuttling out to make the tea.
Nellie's 'Wonderful music', with a request
For 'Wanting You'. Eddie re-installed. Soaring
My mother as my father plunged. And plunged
As his carrot-haired cousin like a seraph soared
In 'Watchman, what of the Night?':

Virginal middle-aged Owen, whose wild eyes
Conveyed the same amazement, whether he prayed
His beloved to come to his arms, in 'Nirvana',
'As the river flows to the ocean',
Or laughed at his own jokes without a sound.
Ethel deaf. None of them, thank God,
For Nirvana this time around.

The Honeymoon Voyage

We have felt lost before,
I tell your mother as the dead
Ship's engines nose through the silent
Mist, and her infirmity
Weakens as home slips further out of reach,
Carn Brea nor Basset Carn, two hills
Of ice slice past us, a monstrous floe

Drifting from Labrador.
The bunk that is our marriage-bed
Pitches through still more violence.
I kiss her tears, confetti
Thrown in a graveyard, her dark eyes beseech
Gentleness I give, our two wills
Melt again into one drifting flow,

And her eyes shine like ore
In the airless cabin. Her head
Lies on my shoulder. In her sigh, love
Leans back to you and pities
Your agony, but we lie each to each,
Wintered yet like your daffodils
Shooting early in the Cornish snow

Moist wind driving ashore
Is beginning to melt. Ahead,
I tell your mother's childlike
Vision, is Yosemite
Again, and the blue rollers of Long Beach,
The small home on Beverly Hills
I built for her, our first car you know

From photographs. Death's more
Beautiful, I tell her, than red-
woods, Sonora's wild lilac,
With a generosity
Warmer than Santa Clara's vale of peach-
trees and apricot, flanked by hills
The golden lemon verbenas grow

So lush on, Livermore . . .
Santa Monica and Merced,
San Francisco's Angel Island,
That creek, Los Alamitos,
Palm Springs . . . Didn't the sight of them outreach
My promise? Remember Soulsbyville's
Strange trees . . . our drive to Sacramento?

Trust me, I tell her, for
The last time I returned I led
You, little more than a child when
We parted, to a city
So wonderful it took away your speech . . .
And she trusts me, while her grief spills
Naturally with the honeymoon snow.

From *Big Deaths, Little Deaths*

I

Late April, '34. Don Bradman drove
to 96, leaving the weary cover
standing, then the day's play was over.
Slept like an angel. Didn't see clouds move
across the stars, eastwards. Westward, love
was blindly choosing out of sperm and ova
two that knit and held. A low cloud-cover
made the ball swing both ways, but the Don clove
cover and mid-off, having read the flight,
and lifted his cap. Something I know as I
was suddenly here that morning—broke
into the universe, I don't know why,
why it was I, on that particular night,
rain starting to fall, her dark field, his dark stroke.

II

Drew a neat hole. Perhaps my uncle, who
had sailed from Cornwall, west, to mine for tin
before he joined the church, was thinking of
the holes he'd drilled to plug explosives in.
Resting on my cricket book, he sketched
an arc. I must have shown my awe. Could jet,
he smiled, half-way across the room.
He flew home to the States. Then the deep snows
of '47; packing, leaving our house,
bound for Australia. Over the round sea
we went. I wept. There were mysterious

lights on the water, white incandescent stars
as I wept for our ginger cat, a man pulled

at the loose tie of a blushing girl's white robe
in the ship's library, I felt a stir, a
fattening ache like tears, a spill of globes.

III

My sister's hubby shooed me from the lounge,
he didn't like the way I watched her thighs
kick off the fat. I didn't like the dark,
it soaked in ghosts and spiders like a sponge,
so took to creeping to my parents' room,
and mother turned out. I slept in father's sweat.

One night the stocky Anzac, a shock ape,
opened their door as I stole past, reeled back.
I was looking for the *Sporting World*, I said.
He loped away to the shower, muttering,
swinging his meat. One day I glimpsed her snatch.
It haunted me for weeks, a mote, a bat.
Asked if I knew about sex, but should have said
Brother I'll show you what it's all about
(I nearly asked her to, it seemed okay)
spreadeagled while the swinging ape was out.

IV

Moon became sun, I came up wet from dreams,
tarantula on the wall, beast on my skin
more terrifying, fat, an atom-bomb.
So much white magic and no stage-assistant,

how could I use this power, if I was in
the flat alone, but breathe her murky scents,
and coil her belt around me, shivering.
A silken, tidal pull like homesickness.
My first affair, intense, unconsummated,
a girl's cool, whispering thighs, a unicorn trapped
in the virgin's lap. Jesus, I choked
in flames I had no way of putting out,
that scorched and tickled in my aching throat.

My padded crop-haired tart, you taught me how
love meshes tighter as it strains apart,
the art of breathing when you're cut in two.

VI

Marlene Dietrich taught me to masturbate,
the blue angel Nazi with her black belt
threw me, as I stood up, threw a switch
enough to jet a rainbow through the screen.
I hobbled to the Cambridge summer evening
and couldn't wait to try it for myself.
Nearly twenty. I developed late.

More deaths than in the purge of Leningrad,
and the siege, under the army blanket,
I learnt the Russian words for tank and shell.
A big girl from an eye infirmary
said tentatively we could try withdrawal,
harpooned on the sofa by my fingers,
but I was scared, I guess, also engaged.

Also she couldn't cure my squint.
Dragging them closer strained my eyes apart.

VII

I rested my forehead against dark glass.
In a lighted window of a facing wing
I saw a nurse brush slowly her long hair.
She must have been thinking of the long
routine ahead, or planning what to wear
for a date. I went back in. The male-nurse
at his wrist guessed it would be ten minutes.

That was twenty years ago. But I do not forget her.
In fact, every day I see her, the slow
stroke of the brush down through her hair, facing
the dark dawn like a mirror; standing there
at the world's end, but wholly unaware,
wholly in the heartless serene world.

XI

They are double-agents exchanged at a border
it's snowing from a grey sky onto black fields
they climb out of black cars

they are terribly tired
of wondering whom they betray
even God does not know whom they betray
they avoid looking into their own eyes

because they have been lovers, or are lovers,
and know only that their hearts are cassette-recorders
and their eyes microfilms, at his hip a pistol
in her black nylon a white ice-pick

yet they won't assassinate—high on cyanide,
implacable tongues nursing the breakable capsules.

Smile

The smile is already there
in the first snap, let's say 17,
under the mop of black
fuzzy ringlets, sitting on the back
steps of a granite cottage
in a Cornish village

the smile is still there
decorative as a film-star
at the wheel of a Model-T
(my father in drainpipe trousers
proudly draped against them both)
in front of a Spanish-white
bungalow in California

and is there, in the same white
place and in the same sunny
era, my sister in her arms,
and is there
under her early-grey hair
sitting on a donkey
on a Cornish beach

and is there
on a bright January day
having tea outside
with her sisters-in-law
and my grandmother
while I stare solemnly
at my first-birthday candle

and the smile is there
under tight white curls

in a Melbourne park,
a plump floral woman
by my plump floral sister
and I a fat youth poking his tongue

and is there, in the last snap
of my father, colour Kodak,
on a Cornish quay, and is there
behind her glasses, hiding pain,
under thinning white hair
on her last holiday with us

and now that she is dead and gone,
having smiled in the undertaker's hut
so I shouldn't feel guilty,
and now that her death has faded
like the snaps,
the smile is still there,
some poems have no beginning and no end.

Ghost-House

I have made a ghost-house of black thread,
black wire. It swings like a birdcage,
a home to house the restless, perturbed dead.
And indeed they have found rest. We both believe
whatever haunts this bedroom with its breath
is breathing quietly and has ceased to grieve.

We think there are two. No, there are squares of two,
infinities of death.
Now while we sleep, the children cannot sleep,
they have to have one too. From their lamp-shade,
black thread and wire, it hangs, as beautiful
and intricate as the one my hands have made.

The Clearing

I make for myself,
or someone makes for me,
a small clearing in my death.
I become a pool
reflecting itself. It is
childhood's pool, utterly clear.

I contemplate it. Who knows
how many years pass?
I look into it, it is full
of sunlight. Who knows
how many years pass?
A waterdrop,

perhaps it is a tear, breaks
the clear water. Circles
spread the pool into
the same pool that turns
into the same pool
and everything the same.
It is childhood's pool, utterly
clear, I am nothing

and I think of nothing.
Once a year I know
it is Good Friday and the pool
is lost. I am broken
into agonised fragments
for three days, then it clears
into the same pool again

and, for a time, something more,
though who it is I am

not certain. I return
to my childhood's pool,
utterly clear. A waterdrop,

perhaps it is a tear, breaks
the clear water, circles
spread the pool into
the same pool, childhood's
pool, I am being cared for
by someone who clearly loves me.

The Handkerchief or Ghost Tree

The Handkerchief or Ghost Tree
stands among Monterey pines,
the Californian redwood, the Chilean
Fire Bush, the Whitebeam, the Maidenhair
Tree, in the Garden of Glendurgan
that slopes to the Helford River,
to the quiet beach of Durgan.

I should remember Durgan.
I was taken here as a child,
many times, and the word 'Durgan'
brought joy to my parents' eyes;
but coming here today, carrying
a child in my arms, I can recognise
nothing of this enchanted
estuary. I can remember only
a flash of pebbles, and being carried
in someone's arms.

When my father died,
and I returned to the hospital
to collect his clothes,
I found in the breast pocket
of his laundered pyjamas
a screwed-up handkerchief
still wringing with the sweat
I had watched pour out of him.

Before he started dying
mysteriously he said:
'My way is clear.'
My sensible Protestant mother

saw a nun, framed
in the bedroom door, warning her
she would always be sleeping alone.

The small child runs
into the garden maze, and vanishes.
We hear his voice, and glimpse
now and again his merry face
through gaps in the laurel.
These lives . . . these lives that come
and go mysteriously, as the laurel-leaves
shine and gloom in the cloudy
sunlight through the tall trees,

this convocation of
the world's trees, massing now
into one, without losing their distinct
character, in the walk down to Durgan.

The Puberty Tree

My puberty tree swayed big, saw-edged leaves
by the open window, and rustled in my sleep
and when I lay awake on the drenched sheet,
for the nights were hot.

I stared at it, whether I woke or slept:
huge black saw-edged leaves against the moonlight.
It pulsed secretly. An immense spider crept
out of it in the dark

and dropped with a light swish into my room:
the Moon-spider, mother of the soft
harmless tarantulas that came inside indeed,
sometimes, and to which

I'd wake in the pale-green dawn or when the fierce
sun was already striking. The puberty tree
spun these black substances out into me,
and also a white

sticky gum I'd find on my chest and belly
in the middle of the night, when my saviour the cool
dawn was a silver-fish in the wall-crack of
a black airless room;

and I lay throbbing, terrified, exalted, strangled,
waiting for the spider-shape to loom.
Night by night the tree went on spinning black
and white substances into me;

now it is wholly inside me: my groin the root,
the slender bough my spine, the saw-edged leaves
my imagination; and the tree sways between
the dark, the light.

III
Anastasia Questioned

From *Marriage of Venice to the Sea on Ascension Day*

1

Gaspara Stampa on the Bridge of Sighs.
No feeling surfaces to her cold form
That she is tortured by this meeting-place.
A hand, bloodied by nails, has drawn across

Light a rich scumble of unclearable cloud,
A golden excrement. Her god had come,
Walked on her waters; rises, vanishes.
His gold ring plunges through immensities

Into the canal whose hymen breaks.
She is left by what she is left with: love.
The artist breaks and re-sets; breaks and re-sets,
Shivering like a chain of gondolas;

From his corruption new perfections rising
To her, as a trained eye finds out new stars.

2

Till choice and chosen are suggested there,
The artist breaks, re-sets, breaks and re-sets
Her arm bent on the linen, troubling his sleep.
In excremental gold the god has come.

Now it is finished save the masterstrokes.
His gold ring plunges through immensities;

With his fingers only he perfects
The hand between her thighs, and draws across

Her upturned gaze the limits of creation.
The hymen is broken and the waters break,
The god-child breasts the breakers. He cleans his hands,

And his trained eye already finds new stars.
He turns the imperfect canvas to the wall,
Where she will find, in darkness now, his love.

3

The Bridge of Tears receives the water-Christ's
Benediction. Greeting the holy form,
In the film of sweat that glistens on her breasts
Each whore has traced with scarlet nails a cross.

Jesus the sun amidst white neophytes.
In golden vesture their God has come,
His gaze fixed high above San Marco's lion
As a god's vision might find out new stars.

The crowds fall to their knees. San Marco booms.
He walks the waters, rises, vanishes.
They jostle, embrace. They have seen the groom's
Gold ring flying through immensities.

The Doge puts out to sea. Gold fetors rising
Light a rich scumble of reflective cloud.

5

They rest, on the Adriatic's bluest skin,
To celebrate a tremulous meeting-place.
The cardinal prays that marriage make them dearer
As a trained eye finds out new stars.

Trumpets. The Doge opens the silver casket.
The hymen is broken and the water breaks.
Under the resettled iconostasis
A gold ring plunges through immensities.

The Doge is moved. He is that mirage
Which walks the waters, rises, vanishes.
Flambeaux flame on the galleys, augment with hymen-
Light the burnt scumble of reflective cloud

Which in the choppier waters, as dusk settles,
An artist breaks, re-sets; breaks, re-sets.

8

A high wind blows in salt to her cloaked face.
Night's hymen's broken, her reflection breaks
Under her. A cannon's boom. Carnival shouts.
The rising flood becomes the meeting-place

Of fireflies and contagion. From her despair,
A phrase. Out of it new perfections rise.
A sonnet begins to live. From the wide sea,
Images, like the Doge's gondolas,

Negotiate into lagoons, canals.
The whole world's waters move through a cold form.
Most flows away again. Poetry's stone

Walks on the waters, rises, vanishes.
Even the flowing out she gathers in,
Building out of all loss a Venice, love.

Sun Valley

It was the first time they had seen the light,
    and gazing, they were too dazed by the sun's
    radiance to murmur when their legs were caught

from under them: with a clean snap of bones
    as they were lifted out, reminding me
    of Yule feasts, or the faint click of a stone's

fall down a chasm. One that had dropped free
    was frightened by a ground so fathomless;
    its wings flapped and its legs flopped uselessly.

More fathomless to my vision was the place
    where they were hung up on the hooks that bare
    them swiftly onwards, upside-down in space;

the cause I know not, but all as they hung there
    let fall a rain of excrement, whence came
    the gross miasma everyone must bear.

How weak are words, and how unfit to frame
    my concept—which lags after what was shown
    so far, it flatters it to call it lame!

And it might be ten thousand fowl or one
    went smoothly past the imperceptible
    electric impulse where they had begun

their afterlife, wings fluttering the while;
    and even after they had been thrust through
    the cutter, headless they were fluttering still.

But swiftly after that their power to move
   compassion vanished—as when, journeying far
   down through Inferno, one's own power to love

vanishes like the sun and the other stars.

Elegy for Isabelle le Despenser

(At Tewkesbury Abbey is a lock of red-brown hair,
belonging to Isabelle, Countess of Warwick, and dated 1429)

Better than stones and castles were my bones.
Better than spears and battles were my tears.
Better than towers and rafters was my laughter.
Better than light and stained glass was my sight.
Better than grate and boar-spit was my hate.
Better than rush and tapestry was my flush.
Better than gold and silver was my shiver.
Better than gloves and falcons was my love.
Better than crests and banners were my breasts.
Better than tombs and effigies was my womb.
Better than art and ikons was my hurt.
Better than crypts and candles were my friendships.
Better than leaf and parchment was my grief.
Better than mass and matins was my chatter.
Better than swans and bridges were my yawns.
Better than wool and weaving was my breathing.

Remember Isabelle le Despenser,
Who was as light and vivid as this hair.
We are all one.
She sees the clouds scud by, she breathes your air,
Pities the past and those who settled there.

Poem in a Strange Language

Starlings, the burnable stages of stars,
Fall back to earth, lightly. And stars,
Propulsars of angels, die in a swift burn.
And half the angels have fallen below the horizon.

And, falling like alpha particles,
Re-charge the drowned woman
Floating in the bitter lake,
Her hair gold as their blood, her face amazed.

She is Lot's wife, her naked body
Sustained by the salt she has loosened from,
And as her eyes open, grain
Turns green-golden on the black earth of Sodom.

I enter your poem, Mandelstam, yours, Anna
Akhmatova, as I enter my love—
Without understanding anything
Except its beauty and law.

And the way its cloud of small
Movements lifts lightly the fruit
Of a painful harvest and moves
With singing vowels away from death.

Poem of the Midway

Where shall we meet, Marina
Tsvetayeva? Have you any
suggestions for our rendezvous?
And in what year?
I shall clutch a photo of you,

but what of the breath
rising and falling under your
coat, your flush, your rumpled
hair? (You'll run from the station.)
What will you wear?

Somewhere midway. Not in your own
city, Moscow. They stole that
from you. Perhaps in Prague,
the embankment, or the café
full of whores and tears
where your love left you—
yes? (I am jealous.)

Somewhere midway. Or I
will come further, let's say 1950
(aren't lovers prone to
pathetic rushed decisions!), ten
years beyond your death, twenty
behind me now. And not
any street that is likely to
rob me of your whole
joy: you will kiss

more beautifully than any,
and I will love you so fiercely

the wild nerves of your poems
will translate straight into my tongue.
Dress for me with the tremulous
awarenesses of the stripped.
(My hand trembles, shaving.)

Our small talk through our night
together! (We won't sleep.)
I know from your poetry
what you think of God, love,
and your life—that suburb
of a town you're exiled from,
but I want to know your tastes
in wine, clothes, films.

Where shall we meet, Marina
Tsvetayeva? Anywhere in Europe
and our century will be dark
enough for our assignation,
and your poems I'll come holding
will give us enough light
to talk by, across a table.
How cool your hand is.

Portraits

(To the memory of Akhmatova)

Nothing visits the silence,
    No apparition of lilac,
        But an inexplicable lightness
            I sense when I breathe your name.
It's not All Souls'. The planet
    Spins on without you, Anna.
        You're now the Modigliani
            Abstract. No candles flame
To amass shadows. Light elected
    You. Annenkov's portrait . . . erect head
        That tilts with a swan's curve
Towards the Neva, towards the living
    Surge of the iced river
        That will not stop nor swerve
But plunge, if need be, within you . . .
    Till room and time started spinning,
        I've gazed, I've tried to splinter
            With love that smiles at stone
This photo of nineteen-twenty,
    The only one where your tender
        Pure and gamine face, grown
One with the page you've entered,
    Blurs at the lips, half-surrenders
        A smile . . . And your lips open
            To me, or familiar Chopin . . .
                It must have been a dream.
But dreams are something substantial,
    The Blue Bird, the soft embalmer.
        It doesn't smell of catacombs
There, and your black fringe is no nimbus.
    A cathedral bell tolls dimly.
        The unmoving stylus hums.

So deep has been this trance,
   Surely its trace fell once,
      Caught your eyes and startled you,
Between the legendary embankment
   And your House on the Fontanka?

     I, like the woman who
Had touched the healer's soul,
   Find everything made whole
     In your poetry's white night,
Envy the poor you kept watch
   With, outside the prison; the touch
     Of a carriage-driver, your slight
Hands bearing down with a spring, one
   Moment in the tense of his fingers.
     Poems outlive a Ming case,
       But your ageing portraits bring me
      The rights of a relative
To grieve. Tonight alone I could spare
   All that is written here
     To restore the chaos where
      The Neva deranges your hair,
       You laugh, weep, burn notes, live.

Lorca

Lorca
walking
in a red-light
district at night
heard one of his own songs
being sung
by a whore

he was moved
as if the stars
and the lanterns
changed places

neither the song
to himself
belonged
nor the girl
to her humiliation
nothing
belonged to anyone

when she stopped singing
it went on

death must be a poor thing
a poor thing

Stone

The first book of a poet should be called *Stone*
Or *Evening*, expressing in a single word
The modesty of being part of the earth,
The goodness of evening and stone, beyond the poet.

The second book should have a name blushing
With a great generality, such as *My Sister Life*,
Shocking in its pride, even more in its modesty:
Exasperated, warm, teasing, observant, tender.

Later books should withdraw into a mysterious
Privacy such as we all make for ourselves:
The White Stag or *Plantain.* Or include the name
Of the place at which his book falls open.

There is also the seventh book, perhaps, the seventh,
And called *The Seventh Book* because it is not published,
The one that a child thinks he could have written,
Made of the firmest stone and clearest leaves,

That a people keep alive by, keep alive.

from *Requiem for Aberfan*

I

'The scenery to the south . . . became surprisingly beautiful . . . noble mountains met the view, green fields and majestic woods.' –George Borrow

Magnates whose sweated legions crucified
The valleys, washed their soft white hands, although
The children died before they died.

Brethren who rode their God in on the tide
Of weeping, hawk this good comfort, that we owe
Our deaths to One on green hill crucified.

The child whose dream, the child whose drawing tried
To tell somebody that the hill would flow,
Knew that they died before they died.

'I dreamt I went to school and there was no school there. Something black had come all over it.' –A victim the day before Aberfan

Workmen who chose and staked this mountainside,
Their ankles lush with streams, a school below,
Learn on what green hill they were crucified.

Sleepers who from their sheets saw the coal slide
And bury, seven nights before it happened, know
The children died before they died.

'Mountains of coal and water were rushing down upon the valley, burying the building. The screams of those children were so vivid I screamed myself.' –A Kent woman's dream

Mothers, whose sharp off-to-death voices denied
Fevers and fancies, following at each cock-crow
The road they drove them to be crucified,

Die on the ninth-hour before they died.

III

There was no keeping out, that day, or keeping in
Either. They set up roadblocks, but you couldn't stop

All Britain pitching in and trying to help.
Or gawp. I stopped one car myself, a whole family,
From the Midlands. 'Is this the place where all
    those kids
Are buried?' he said. But mostly they wanted to help,
Anything they could do. Which wasn't much.
They didn't have a chance, you see, didn't have
    a chance . . .
Yet, you couldn't seem to keep them in. The children.
Not all that lot could. My missus and me,
    we saw David
A score of times, I suppose, that Friday.
    He was everywhere!
Running up to the front-door, about to bang it shut,
About to turn the corner. Always *about* to, always
    three of us,
In the road, in the crowd. Once, I still swear
    I *did* see him,
In Moy Road, then he vanished. There were the
    rumours, you see,
Of some being found alive. The whole terrace
    was like that,
Full of them. No, you couldn't shut them in.
    It was like
Holes in the slurry you couldn't see. There were
More kids about the place than normal, I'd say.
Funny, it was the same even when I'd found David
In Bethania. Not a mark on him, there wasn't.
    Like a doll.
We still hoped. It hadn't happened, do you know?

IV

The Father

The day you came, I felt her turn from me.
Absence, fullbreasted, coasting at my side,
Straining for different hungers—rightfully.

With no regrets, my pit-black spirit died
And rose like waste through galleries of you.
Cast like a tip, I saw and sang my pride,

The first-born, inexhaustible, the new
Seam, richer, deeper than all Rhondda. A man
Gets born again out of his wife, I knew,

What did it matter that the more you ran
Into your mother's heart, the closer I felt
To an eighth spewed cone outtopping Aberfan?

With no regrets. And yet have I not knelt
Begging God that His curse should overwhelm
Breaths held in, ears strained   Me also, so confirmed was I in guilt
for a faint murmur that
would lead to a life saved.
Silence . . . the whistle again,
digging resumed.   At having willed this on you, in some dream
I had forgotten maybe. When, as the arc-
Lights flickered on the ant-hill, I heard your scream

Rise faintly from a desk, miles deep, the black
Slurry was in myself. Why did we pause?
Now, when the shuddering cage transports us back

Deputies and over-men kept the few details to themselves. They did not want panic. There was none, but no man came to the surface without knowing why. There are no secrets underground.

To that rise up to hell—untold, we knew—
Always I hear, faintly, unreachably,
You cry where my own evil fell on you.

V

The Brother

I steal into his room, with my pack of cards,
And play patience under his photo,
Hoping to tempt him.
I get tired of it. It never comes out.

So I go to the mountain, quite a lot.
I remember we had a story once
About how somebody led these children into the
    mountain,
And there was a lame boy who couldn't go.

He dreams of his elder brother having parties in the grave.

Mummy doesn't know, but they have parties in the
    grave.
Last night, in my sleep, I heard it.
I was in disgrace for telling on them, but I didn't.
Robert called me Sissy.

'Robert, Robert, play with me. You can win.'

The terrace is empty. All summer it's Sunday.
If I showed him my cards, offered to let him win
Only so he would play with me, play,
Would he let me in?

VI
The Doll

I should have seen her. I might accept it, resign
Myself to having lost her. Not now. You can't
Send your child off to school at nine
O'clock and never see her again. You *can't*!

Diane could move her head
now; she turned, saw the
child who sat next to her. She
screamed: 'That's my sister.'
'No, dear, it's a dolly.' Dr
Oliver threw a blanket over
the dolly. Diane went quiet.

The wouldn't let me into Bethania, where
They had taken her. I should have fought my way in.
They seemed to think I wouldn't be able to bear
It. The condition she was in.

Because of that, she lives. I put flowers
On her grave like the rest, every day,
                                          but she's not there,
Not to me she isn't. It has blue eyes like hers—
Look how they open. To me she's there,

Shut inside the doll. It was her best doll.
I say, Try, darling, try to move
Your arms and legs for me, try. But it's all
That stuff, surrounding, binding. She never moves.

But I can see her struggling. It's such a shame,
All that blackness round them . . . Sometimes her eyes
Flinch open up at me as though I'll blame
Her for not escaping. As though her eyes

Can see me, either! But there is always hope
That one day . . . And so I keep the room

101

Exactly as she left it—her books, her skipping-rope,
Her nightclothes. Suppose she woke to a strange
    room?

People don't like it. Callers say I should free
Myself from the past, that I must forget.
My freedom's here in this room. She grew from me:
Who would remember her if I forgot?

VIII
Committal

Earth trapped our shadows also as we leant
Over the slit-trench.
Bodies saw them die.
Yet when we drifted down the path
—Buoyed up breathless, half-conscious, by
    communal loss,
As if lifted off our feet by a great crowd
Out of Cardiff Arms Park—
Our bodies stayed behind, our shadows went.

IX
The Quickening

The year turns, to the eve. She lies awake.

The third week of October 1966 was notable for high winds and heavy rain.

Once more the storm comes slanting out of the west.
The younger girl is breathing by her side.
Even so, that night, black drops had slashed the pane.

102

She flinches; at this hour her child had cried
Out in her sleep, but she has calmed her fears.
She hears the tip upbristling, stormed awake.

Silently, she rises. There are fears
Of rain the spirit in the doll cannot
Express. She crosses the dim passageway,
to comfort it. But it is cold; so trapped!

Parents needed to have chil-
dren near. Mothers slept with
daughters and fathers with
sons. Normal marital rela-
tions were interrupted.

She bears it downstairs, opens the door, to lay
Her burden in the fury of the storm.
Crying, the storm lacerates her tears.

She mounts. And goes this time into his room.
She melts into his dream of wind and rain.
She hears the loud drops guttering from the eaves
Upon the lonely doll, running the stiff wax,
Releasing limbs beflagged with torn wet leaves,
And as the rain drums on, the quickening breach,
She feels her child's return within her womb.

X

The red lights of Tip Number 7 gleam through the
    dusk,
Shutting the stable. It is Christmas. Except in
    Aberfan.
I stand in the mountainside cemetery, handblowing,
    cold.
The school is here,
Pantglas School eternally in session.

The master arrived, the names called, and the register
    collected.
Dyfrig, David, Janette, Kelvyn . . .
Incorrigible, they are now corrected,
Wilful, in line.

Not requiem, not rest—
Unrest, mischievousness!
Have them break ranks,
Somewhere, somewhere, a boy set rebellion going!
Dissolve this petrifaction of scripture
Into games, into movement;
Release them to a playground's anarchy.
They have won well their omegas, their black stars,
Their death's word-perfect:
They are impatient to say it over, and go.
I would say
Learn, you too-rigid, you too-silencing teacher,
That children can't concentrate
On any subject, can't concentrate
Past bell and alarum, can't concentrate,
As these are doing,
For long.

Whale

A whale lay cast up on the island's shore
    in the shallow water of the outgoing tide.
        He struggled to fill his lungs,
        he grew acquainted with weight.

And the people came and said, Kill it, it is food.
And the witch-doctor said, It is sacred, it must not be harmed.
And a girl came and with an empty coconut-shell
    scooped the seawater and let it run over the whale's blue bulk.

A small desperate eye showing white all round
    the dark iris. The great head flattened against
        sand as a face pressed against glass.

And a white man came and said, If all the people
    push we can float it off on the next tide.
And the witch-doctor said, It is taboo, it must not be touched.

And the people drifted away.
And the white man cursed and ran off to the next village for help.

And the girl stayed.
She stayed as the tide went out.
The whale's breath came in harsh spasms.
Its skin was darkening in the sun.
The girl got children to form a chain
of coconut-shells filled with fresh water
that she poured over his skin.

The whale's eye seemed calmer.

With the high tide the white man came back.
As the whale felt sea reach to his eye he reared
on fins and tail flukes, his spine arced

and he slapped it all down together, a great leap
into the same inert sand.
His eye rolled
in panic as again he lifted and crashed down,
    exhausted, and again lifted and crashed down,
        and again, and again.

The white man couldn't bear his agony and strode away,
    as the tide receded.
He paced and paced the island and cursed God.

Now the whale didn't move.
The girl stroked his head
and as the moon came up
she sang to him
of friends long dead and children grown and gone,
sang like a mother to the whale,

and sang of unrequited love.

And later in the night
    when his breaths had almost lost touch
        she leant her shoulder against his cheek

and told him stories, with many details,
of the mud-skipping fish that lived
        in the mangroves on the lagoon.

Her voice
and its coaxing pauses
was as if fins
were bearing him up to the surface of the ocean
to breathe and see,
as with a clot of blood falling on her brow
the whale passed clear from the body of his death.

The Dream Game

There was a black girl
who was so beautiful all the white men slept with her.
She had a hunter, an analyst, a manufacturer, and a poet.
And so clever
she picked up their language from their conversations.

She grew unhappy as
she couldn't dream, and not to dream was a kind of
constipation to the black girl, a growing burden
she grew fat with,
so that they had to buy her a pantigirdle.

We'll make you a dream,
said the analyst, and you must guess what it is.
When she had gone he explained to the others, smiling,
they wouldn't make up a dream
for the black girl, she would make up her own.

If her questions, if her guesses,
he said, contain in the last word the letter e, say yes,
if not, say no. The hunter, the manufacturer,
and the poet smiled,
and they called the black girl back into the room.

They instructed her
to ask them each in turn a question about the dream
they had made up for her. She could go on questioning
for as long as
she liked. It was important she find her dream.

How their laughter
exploded at her frequent marvellous guesses.

Black girl, they said, this is black magic! and their
beer spluttered out
of their mouths in uncontrollable mirth as she

unwound her dream, her dream
that all four of them had murdered her with knives,
cut her up in the kitchen, and re-cycled her
into trees, into paper
on which beautiful elegies were written about her.

Diary of a Myth-Boy

Something called Death came today. Witch-
doctor has this big dream,
tells him three canoes sailing down-
stream, Immortal Spirit
in third one. So he lines us all up.
Sure enough, about noon,
canoe comes, full of rotten fruit.
That's Death, says the witch-doctor. White
man comes sailing down in
second canoe, and our stupid
sod of a witch-doctor
wades out and embraces him! Down
comes Immortal Spirit in third
canoe, waving his arms
shouting, That's Death, you fool, can't you
even count up to three?
He just stood, scratching his head and
grinning, he's not all there . . .

Grandmother comes to me in the
night, squats on my face and
farts. If you ask me she's crazy.
This afternoon sharpened
my arrow-heads . . .

                    Followed mother
when she went out gathering
palms to make my penis-sheath. Saw,
as she climbed to the top,
my first cunt, rich as a date. Raped
her. Told grandmother. She
said, You're a big boy now, but watch

out for your father. If he
sends you to the region of souls,
take a hummingbird with
you. Crazier and crazier . . .

Sick all morning. Could this
be pregnancy or grandmother's
farts? My father in a
terrible temper, tells me to
set out tomorrow for
the region of souls, to fetch a
dance-rattle. Sure thing my
mother's ratted on me, the cow . . .

Grandmother's dead. When she
came last night I stuck an arrow
up her arse. Her guts fell
out. God, she was rotten. No more
entries for a few days.
Lots to write about, I expect,
when I come back . . .

                    Granny
was right about the hummingbird.
Dance-rattle hung from a
cord, hummingbird's beak cut it. It
splashed into the river,
alerted the souls who fired their
arrows in. If I'd been
there I wouldn't be writing this,
Dance-rattle floated to
me. Grandmother wise woman. When

I got home, mother and
sister, sick, father away hunting
—I'd like to have seen that
bastard's face. No food cooked . . .

Mother and sister dead, with most
of the other women.
Sister goes to my hut to fetch
dead fish, takes granny's guts
instead. Stupid bitch! It's poison
of course. Everyone who
ate it died. They call it Disease.
Saves me the bother of
killing mother for tale-telling . . .

No girls left. We boys muck
about among ourselves. We're all
pregnant but can't bear kids.
It's no fun cooking and cleaning,
and with fat bellies too.
What a life! . . .

                    Got my revenge on
father today. Put on
antlers, met him out hunting, speared
him. Flung him in the lake.
Spirits must have got him, his lungs
floated up . . .

                    Saw this girl,
up a tree, the first for bloody
months. Chatted her up, it

turned out she didn't like fish. I
tried to climb the trunk but
my erection got in the way,
came all over it and
gave up. A crowd of the other
lads came at her through the
treetops, raped her, then cut her up
into little pieces.
Which, as they slid down the trunk, met
my sperm and of course turned
into girls. I got a thick slice
of rump and my girl's well
stacked. Some of them are skin and bone . . .

God it's a boring life,
no tribes to fight with, all killed off
by Disease (grandmother
started something there), my
fat wife a pain in the arse. A
white anthropologist
who's turned up here's been telling me
about life with his folk.
It sounds really exciting. I'm
going to pack a few
pearls and things tonight, slip this
diary under the
anthropologist's tent-flap and
sneak away up river . . .

Vienna. Zürich. Constance

It was a profound unmeeting.
The train on the branchline from Zürich to Constance
Held a carriage which held a compartment
With a white seat-cover with an impression of Dr Jung,
Slit eyes, in a pugnacious bullet head,
By no means the merry young man of his old age.

The young woman opposite, bright
In a black-and-white striped dress, a blue neck-scarf,
Did not chat to the man not clutching his brief-case
But read through the short journey, smiling occasionally,
Nor did she follow him out at Constance
Where he was warmly embraced by an older man.

The train on the branchline from Constance to Zürich
Held a carriage which held a compartment
With a white seat-cover with an impression of Dr Freud,
His face graven with battles, genial-eyed.
The young man opposite in a modern, very
Tight brown suit with a heavy Victorian watch-chain

Was not startled by the old gent not leaning forward
And not telling him with a twinkle why he had stammered
Momentarily over the word Constance,
But rubbed his hands dreamily and gazed out.
Nor did he help him with his case at Zürich
Where he was greeted cordially by his son.

By a strange coincidence
The young woman who would have been in Jung's compartment,
Had Jung been travelling, was the mistress
Of the young man who would have been in Freud's compartment

Had Freud been travelling. Having confused
Their plans, they passed each other, unaware.

Waiting for him in her hotel at Constance,
The young woman stepped out of her rainy clothes.
Her fur hat momentarily became a vulva.
Waiting for her in his hotel at Zürich,
The young man stared irritably out of the window
And saw an uncanny light pass across the sky.

Emma and the children leaving the table,
The sage head darkly reflected in its polish
Did not gracefully accept the modified libido theory.
Gazing into the waters of Lake Constance,
A fatherly hand resting on his shoulder,
Jung did not smilingly abjure his mystical drift.

Freud dined sombrely with the faithful Binswanger,
And pleaded a headache. Jung worked late. Owls hooted.
In their uneasy sleep the two exchanged their dreams.
Snow fell on the Jungfrau. Lenin dreamlessly slept.
The centuries slowly drifted away from each other.
In Emma's kitchen-drawer a knifeblade quietly snapped.

Fathers, Sons and Lovers
(Vienna, 1919)

Tausk – Freud (letter)

Dear Freud. I have arranged to go at one
daily to Frau Deutsch. She is yours at three,
I gather, and at noon she feeds her son.
Your letter came as a surprise to me,
I must confess. I fear I had presumed,
in view of my long service to the cause
and, above all, to you, you'd have assumed
the burden of my analysis. I was
a little shaken, wondering what offence
I'd given. But since you've taken her
yourself, a rare mark of her excellence
in your regard, I'm calmer, happier
about unmasking my mind's violence.

Freud – Helene Deutsch (analysis)

She thanks you for the goat's milk. Bring your son,
now he is weaned, to visit her some time—
my wife would like that; stop her brooding on
my careless ash! . . . A candle in a lime-
tree: beautiful, so rich! I catch a gleam
of light, at last, at last. I think we ought
to keep on, after all. And yet you seem
held back still, somehow. When you came, I caught
a scent—yes, yes, I know—but more like musk.
Don't let him drain you of all energy.
How near the end are you? Take care. His tusk
has ploughed through women before, to get to me.
They're not the fruit he craves, simply the husk.

Helene Deutsch—Lou Salomé (letter)

I bring you greetings from my mother-in-law;
you were a fellow-student, I believe.
Your paper, last night, on dementia
was brilliant; I regret I had to leave
before the end—my child was ill. I write
to plead with you to use your influence
with Freud. I know my stumbling thoughts are trite,
but he can't keep awake. I have a sense
of sickness, self-destructive gloom. Please make
him rest a little, take a holiday.
He seems afraid of Tausk. I cannot break
that man's resistance. Compelling, though, the way
his eyes flash up and hold one, like a snake!

Lou Salomé—Freud

In Russia, with my husband and my lover,
I sensed, beneath our private turbulence,
a violence the deep ice could not cover,
and I am not surprised by these events.
Rilke was plunged in gloom. I gave him there
the symbol that he later used so well—
a panther circling endlessly its despair.
I sense it now in Tausk—an animal.
You know the unimaginable splendour
men can invest a hair, a shoe, a glove;
yet Tausk—so good a soul—will not surrender,
even to himself, the covenant of his love,
and so is cruellest where he feels most tender.

116

Freud–Lou Salomé

How the still night conceals Vienna's hurts!
I love the lights reflecting on the water,
our quiet strolls, the rustle of your skirts.
Yes, talk to Anna, if you would; my daughter
should be less tied to me. My friend, our talks
heal me at day's end. I'm hacking through
a lonely, perilous jungle. Nietzsche stalks
there too, ahead. And Rilke–yes. Frau Lou,
I'd like to rest, but too much is at stake.
I feel my age. The death-wish theory rose
out of a dream I had. A small grass snake
punctures my brow and, as I weaken, grows.
A python haunts the path it knows I'll take.

Lou Salomé–Tausk (letter)

My friend, what can I say? Poor Victor! Brother-
animal! The life of a great man is fraught,
demonic. Freud could not endure another
creative mind frustrating his own thought.
Unquestioningly she would obey him–so
besotted is she. Think: poor *Sigmund*! Is
it not, after all, more moving than chilling to know
he has reached greatness through his frailties?
Think of your bride-to-be; you're not alone.
And though I slept with you because you were
close to the master, as you must have known,
you'll find no friend who's truer, tenderer.
That was our house of straw, but this is stone.

Tausk—Freud (letter)

Kindly give aid to Fräulein Loewi, one
created to be a pure and loving wife.
I would have failed her, as I failed, as son
and father, lover and husband, all my life.
I must do this thing right, and to that end
will noose the curtain-cord around my throat
and put the pistol to my brow. My friend,
dying is good, it is an antidote
to all our ills, it is great joy to climb
out of my animal skin. The linden trees
are singing. For everything, I thank you; I'm
honoured that I knew you. Yours. Tausk. Please,
also look after my sons from time to time.

Peter Kürten to the Witnesses
(Düsseldorf, 1931)

I have too much a sense of being alive
to take the guillotine in another way
than as the cause of an erection.
I've lived, dreading reprieve, anticipating
the ecstasy of hearing my own blood gush.
It's true, and I don't want pity.

One night I roamed the Hofgarten lake,
in a desperate condition, but found only a swan,
and cut its head off while it slept.
It's chilly. I won't be long. If I were you
I'd be anticipating the orgasm, like the day
I saw a mangled horse.

I can smell blood a mile off and I'm certain
the hour is at hand when you will say,
Why did we kill good Peter Kürten?
But it's as well. I should be much too soft;
for the time came when I grew tired,
felt I could do no more.

I'm sorry about the children, and especially
little Gertrude, she took my hand so trustingly.
I loved children and they loved me.
As the Prosecutor said, I am—I am—
I am rather a nice man. And a shy man.
My stammer gets worse when I'm keyed up. I'm sorry.

I desperately wanted all the women who came
with me, so willingly, not to be upset
but to share the pleasure, to share

the absurd comedy of my dropping behind
on the path, lassoing them suddenly, dragging
them over the earth.

Everyone's been most kind. I've put on weight.
If I was free, I'd kill you all. All Düsseldorf
still wouldn't be enough.
And yet, you know, there were times I dreamed
I'd capture the Monster, and be fêted
by my grateful fellow-citizens!

You're welcome to my brain, gentlemen
of the University; I'll think of you
slicing it like tripe, saying
There's Maria Hahn, and there's Rose Ohliger,
etcetera, etcetera, and here is our answer.
But that would surprise me.

I could tell you it was my father raping
my mother and my sister, ten of us in one room,
or being taught to torture
and masturbate dogs, but it's deeper than that,
it's what I am, through eternity, therefore
I must thank God who doesn't exist.

Be good to my wife. She never knew the mayhem in
our bed. That was heroic of me. I wrote
last night to all the next-of-kin.
I'm grateful also for the many fine loveletters
women have sent to me—perhaps your own wives.
Thank you for seeing me off.

The House of Dreams

It is a good house, and made of teak,
surrounded by a forest. Behind the deep-freeze
a bushmaster may surprise you, surprised.

It is a honeymoon hotel
visited by the dead and the living.
They share the same taxis, and a fool
has muddled all the reservations.
They love you. They are to be loved.

Jesus is in the manger. Shepherds have come.
It is something about loving everyone
and you may be surprised
that the casually dropped invitation
has been taken up, twenty years later.

In an ornate bar-room with purple drapes
there is a negress in a black corset
playing the piano. There is croquet
and television, and a room for loneliness.

Sappho is there, and Jung, and Freud,
and the girl you shared a train journey with,
who leaned out of the window and said,
'I wish you were coming with me.'
They love you. They are to be loved.
Lola Montez is dancing to the negress.

Farewell, My Life;
I Love You

1

Your letter has touched me with its simple meaningless phrases,
its strokes as clear as stars in this summer sky,
as pointless and serene, my love, my fate.
Beneath the absolute beauty of your surfaces
there is nothing, nothing, Natalia. That is why
I love you. To love you is to learn to skate.

The deepest thing about you is your pearls,
those creatures of the sea who rest between
the marble, soft, exquisite, lifeless mountains
—my hermitages, after the soulful girls
whose kisses were quicker than lizards in green
gardens of fig-trees and eternal fountains.

I love the emptiness of your smile, your slow
wit, your foolish chatter. A child, I play
in your suburban street, before carriages
and crowds have smutched it, after the first snow;
you dazzle me, and that is how you'll stay
after many childbearings and miscarriages.

I shall come to you without fail, in autumn, soon.
Do you understand? I shall come at the year's fall.
My name is the only word I need to hear—
without turning to me your face, the vapid moon.
It is miracle enough that you speak at all
or comb at all your magnificent black hair.

I hunger for you to touch me absently;
your tolerant indifference does not hurt
any more. I will hover above you

hoping for a sign of life in your perfectly
still face, but happy to feel your beating heart.
Farewell, my life; I love you.

2

Dizzily the pines fly past;
sorrowful, the confused soul
is half determined to turn back
along the already buried track,
but fearfully out of control
she is borne on by the sleigh's
joyful momentum and the hollow
ache in her throat she cannot swallow.

It's silent. Round the only rays,
maddened, helpless in the circle
of its unrest, the blizzard swarms;
her eyes are hot as candleflames;
the sky is heavy with the weight
of whiteness deepening the night;
she thinks the way ahead is home,
the girl is in delirium;
now she is losing consciousness;
but the sleigh sings on cracking ice,
knowing the water to be crossed,
knowing her longing to be lost
in love tonight and sacrificed.

Anastasia Questioned

I don't know who I am. Perhaps I am
the ikon lamp they lit for me at birth,
the pure gold, melted down to feed
all the poor people on the poor earth.
I have been bled white as Alexei's skin,
as the white sky behind these winter trees
meshed beyond identity. I'm in
a nightmare where I wake to a bad room,
making the sign of the cross, embracing each other,
waiting for death to come, the bolshevik.
I am all the poor people on the poor earth.
I am not what I say, and yet the sea
cannot contain the tears
that have blotted out my memory.
I am the charred clothes and the severed finger,
corset-bones underground and the pet dog.
I'm the dumb girl dragged out of a canal,
and I am running towards trees,
raped by my captors, struck violent blows.
I'm in a closed train heading for Kazan
with Mama and my sisters. Mama! Marie!
Where are you? I am wherever you are.
I'm in the family group of peasants by
the woodpile Papa has just chopped up.
We're smiling, huddled, and the picture snows.
The century's stretched me out, a flight of cranes,
no landmark in the featureless snow reminds
me of my name.

Life has touched me like Rasputin's kiss
and I'm too simple-minded to be sure
I don't survive. I think I am the wind

playing around the entrance to the shaft
over which four pine-trees used to thresh
called the Four Brothers. I am the spirit-lamp
I dressed by at Ipatiev, shivering,
the clock that went on ticking, burnt to ash.

Notes

p. 19   *Logan Stone.* The Logan Stone is a finely-balanced granite boulder on the cliffs near Land's End in Cornwall. To 'log', in old Cornish, is to set trembling.

p. 22   *Sonoran Poems.* 'Kachina' (Pueblo-Navajo): any form concealing a god's presence. 'The lord's candles': yucca blossoms.

p. 26   *The Book of Changes.* Based on the hexagrams of the Chinese *I Ching.*

p. 31   *Weddings.* After Catullus LXII.

p. 39   *Don Giovanni.* From *The White Hotel,* a novel. The narrator, a patient of Freud's, has fantasied an affair with one of his sons.

p. 47   *Penwith.* The name of the most westerly outcrop of Cornwall, on which many ancient stone monuments are scattered: including a circle of boulders known as the Merry Maidens, and the men-an-tol ('holed stone'), through which one crawled to cure rickets or other ills.

p. 48   *Botallack.* Also near Land's End; a disused tin-mine set into the cliff. 'Bal', or 'mine', maidens were the women who broke up ('spalled') the rocks, in the nineteenth century. Another image refers to the legend of Lyonesse, a kingdom lost beneath the sea. One man, riding a white horse, is supposed to have fled east and escaped the flood.

p. 49   *Meditation on Lines from the Methodist Hymnal.* Tin was being mined in Cornwall, and sold to foreign traders, before the Chris-

127

tian era. There is a legend that Joseph of Arimathea was a tin-trader, and on one of his voyages he brought the boy Jesus. 'Knackt bal': a worked-out mine. 'Kerensa': the ancient Celtic-Cornish word for love.

p. 60   *A Cornish Graveyard at Keweenaw.* Like the Irish, the Cornish emigrated in large numbers to America during the last century. The mining communities retained their clannish identity. Unlike the Welsh, the Cornish were and are 'hard-rock' miners: tin, copper, iron, silver, gold, quicksilver.

p. 62   *Under Carn Brea.* Carn Brea is a granite hill in West Cornwall, overlooking the village where I was born.

p. 65   *The Honeymoon Voyage.* My father went to California to find work when he was nineteen. Four years later, in 1923, he came home briefly to marry my mother. They were married on Easter Saturday morning, saw a rugby match in the afternoon, and sailed for America in the evening.

p. 67   *Big Deaths, Little Deaths.* Don Bradman: Australia's greatest cricketer. When he opened the Australian tour of England in 1934 with his usual big score at Worcester, I – further west – was being conceived: or so I reckon. At fourteen, I went to Australia with my parents and spent two years there.

p. 83   *Marriage of Venice to the Sea on Ascension Day.* Gaspara Stampa (1523–54) wrote her most intense love-sonnets not long before her death, and in the year of Titian's Danae and the Golden Shower. One of the sonnets, which lament her lover's desertion, concludes: 'He in whom I find new perfections, As a trained eye finds out new stars'.

p. 87   *Sun Valley.* The name of a chicken-factory in Hereford, England.

p. 91   *Poem of the Midway.* Marina Tsvetayeva (1892–1941) emigrated to the West after the Russian Revolution; she returned to Russia in 1939, endured great suffering and loneliness, and took her life. One of her best-known works is a sequence of tragic love-poems called *Poem of the End*.

p. 93   *Portraits.* Anna Akhmatova (1889–1966) survived the Stalinist Terror, during which her son was arrested and sent to Siberia. The portrait by Modigliani was painted when she visited Paris before the First World War. The form of my poem echoes the metre of the major work of her later years, *Poem Without a Hero.*

p. 97   *Requiem for Aberfan.* On October 21, 1966, in the Welsh coal-mining village of Aberfan, Tip Number 7, containing waste or slurry from the mine, slipped and overwhelmed Pantglas Junior School. Twenty-eight adults and 116 children were killed: a generation. The marginal glosses in the sequence are from *Aberfan,* a book by Tony Austin, and from a BBC television documentary.

p. 105   *Whale.* After an incident in Lyall Watson's book *Gifts of Unknown Things.*

p. 109   *Diary of a Myth-Boy.* Based on myths of Central Brazil.

p. 113   *Vienna. Zürich. Constance.* In May 1912 Freud visited the town of Constance, near Zürich, to spend a weekend with a sick colleague. Jung was deeply hurt that he had not taken the opportunity to visit him in Zürich; Freud equally so that the younger man had not come to see him in Constance. Their relationship, already strained, ended abruptly soon after.

p. 115   *Fathers, Sons and Lovers.* Victor Tausk, 1879–1919, was one of Freud's most talented and experienced followers. After a decision that all analysts must themselves be analysed, Freud appointed Helene Deutsch to analyze Tausk. At Freud's prompting, she broke off Tausk's analysis mid-way. Deprived of his last frail link with the master, Tausk committed suicide. The fourth person in the poem, Lou Andreas-Salomé, was the gifted friend or mistress of Nietzsche, Rilke, Freud, and Tausk.

p. 119   *Peter Kürten to the Witnesses.* When Kürten, the notorious mass-murderer, was arrested and tried, the liberal German government agonised over whether he should be executed. The guillotine, in fact, had become rusted from disuse.

p. 122   *Farewell, My Life; I Love You.* The title occurs, as a valediction, in a letter from Pushkin to his wife, Natalia.

– D.M.T.

ACKNOWLEDGMENTS

The poems in this selection have been taken from the following volumes:

Modern Poets 11 (Penguin, 1968): "Cygnus A."

Two Voices (Cape Goliard, London, and Grossman Publishers/The Viking Press, New York, 1968): "Wolfbane," "A Lesson in the Parts of Speech," "Requiem for Aberfan."

Logan Stone (Cape Goliard, London, and Grossman Publishers/The Viking Press, New York, 1971): "Computer 70," "Haiku Sequence," "Trawl," "Lakeside," "Logan Stone," "Penwith," "Botallack," "Meditation on Lines from the Methodist Hymnal."

Love and Other Deaths (Paul Elek Ltd., London, 1975): "Cecie," "Reticent," "Dream," "Rubble," "Marriage of Venice to the Sea on Ascension Day," "Poem of the Midway," "Poem in a Strange Language," "Friday Evening," "You Are on Some Road," "Sonoran Poems," "The Book of Changes."

The Honeymoon Voyage (Secker & Warburg Ltd., London, 1978): "The Dream Game," "Whale," "Ninemaidens," "A Cornish Graveyard at Keweenaw," "Under Carn Brea," "The Honeymoon Voyage," "Flesh," "Weddings," "Portraits," "Elegy for Isabelle le Despenser," "Lorca," "Stone," "Vienna. Zürich. Constance," "Diary of a Myth-Boy."

Dreaming in Bronze (Secker & Warburg, Ltd., London, 1981): "Farewell, My Life; I Love You," "Fathers, Sons and Lovers," "Peter Kürten to the Witnesses," "Anastasia Questioned," "Big Deaths, Little Deaths," "Smile," "Ghost-House," "Two Women, Made by the Selfsame Hand," "Poetry and Striptease," "The House of Dreams," "Sun Valley," "The Clearing," "The Handkerchief or Ghost Tree," "The Puberty Tree," "Blizzard Song."

"Vienna. Zürich. Constance" first appeared in *The American Scholar*.

Three poems in *Dreaming in Bronze* ("Ghost-House," "The House of Dreams," and "The Clearing") first appeared in the novel *Birthstone* (1980). Grateful acknowledgment is made to Victor Gollancz Ltd., London, for permission to reprint these poems.

Acknowledgment is also made to Victor Gollancz Ltd., London, and Viking Penguin Inc., New York, for permission to reprint part of "Don Giovanni" from *The White Hotel*.

D. M. Thomas was born in Cornwall, England, in 1935. He was educated there, in Australia, and at New College, Oxford. He has been a teacher and lecturer, and is now a full-time writer. His first novel, *The Flute-Player*, won the Gollancz/Pan/Picador Fantasy Award. His most recent novel, *The White Hotel*, which received the 1981 Cheltenham Prize, the *Los Angeles Times* Fiction Prize, and the P.E.N. Fiction Prize, is an international best-seller. He has published five volumes of verse, including *The Honeymoon Voyage* and *Dreaming in Bronze*; he is also well known for his translations of Russian poetry, including *The Bronze Horseman: Selected Poems of Alexander Pushkin*. He has three children and lives in Hereford, England, where he has just completed his fourth novel, *Ararat*.